Robots
ACTIVITY BOOK

SUSAN SHAW-RUSSELL

DOVER PUBLICATIONS, INC.
MINEOLA, NEW YORK

Copyright

Copyright © 2009 by Dover Publications, Inc.
All rights reserved.

Bibliographical Note

Robots Activity Book is a new work, first published by Dover
Publications, Inc., in 2009.

International Standard Book Number
ISBN-13: 978-0-486-47227-0
ISBN-10: 0-486-47227-2

Manufactured in the United States by Courier Corporation
47227201
www.doverpublications.com

Note

What's full of nuts and bolts and a ton of fun—robots! In this activity book you will find all different types of robots including Roddy who runs on electricity, brother and sister robots Riley and Roxy, robotic pets Max and Holly, and even Reggie the solar powered robot. There are counting games, word searches, connect-the-dots, spot-the-differences, mazes, and other activities that will provide you with many hours of fun. And after you're through solving all the puzzles, you can color them any way you choose! If you need help with a puzzle, or if you want to check your answers, the solutions begin on page 53.

Find and circle the letters that spell "ROBOT" hidden in this picture.

Roddy Robot runs on electricity. Circle the outlet in which his plug will fit.

Here are 2 pictures of Raymond and Roxy Robot. Add 5 things to the top picture so that it matches the bottom one exactly.

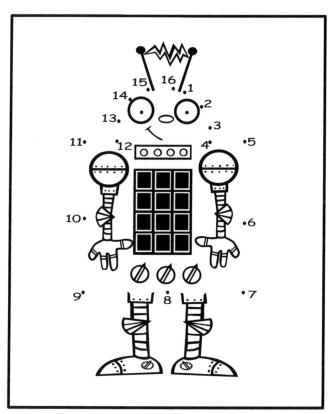

Connect the dots to see what Reggie the Robot looks like.

Help the robots count the nuts. Then circle the tool box with that number on it.

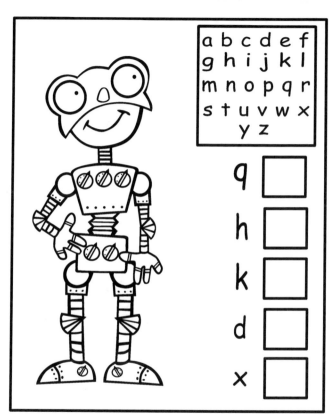

a b c d e f	
g h i j k l	
m n o p q r	
s t u v w x	
y z	

q [ ]
h [ ]
k [ ]
d [ ]
x [ ]

In each empty box, write in the letter that
comes after the one beside it, (use the complete
alphabet to help), and you'll know the name
of this robot.

Connect the dots to see what Max the robotic dog looks like.

To find out the names of these two robots, circle the first nut and then every other one after that. Then fill in the blanks with the circled letters.

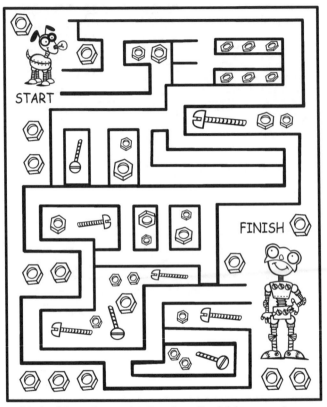

Help Max the robotic dog find his way to Riley Robot.

Color in the picture of Riley and his sister
Roxy and their dog Max.

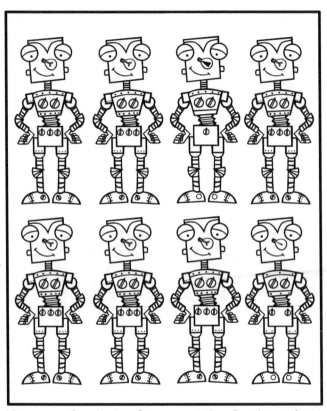

Here are 8 robots. Cross out the 2 robots that look different from the other robots.

Connect the dots to see what Holly the robotic cat looks like.

r=1 u=2 a=3 s=4 f=5 n=6
d=7 o=8 e=9 m=10 Y=11

__ __ __ __ __   __ __ __
1 2 5 2 4   3 6 7

__ __ __ __ __ __ __ __
1 8 4 9 10 3 1 11

Use the number code to discover the names of
these two robots. Write the letters in the blanks
provided.

Color in this picture of Max and Holly
the robotic pets.

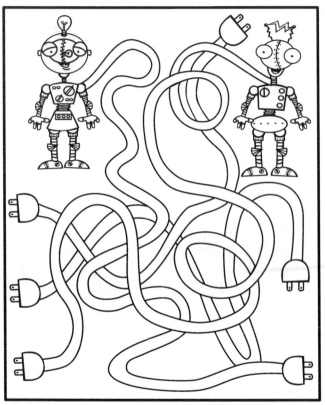

Follow the cords from each of the robots to their plugs.

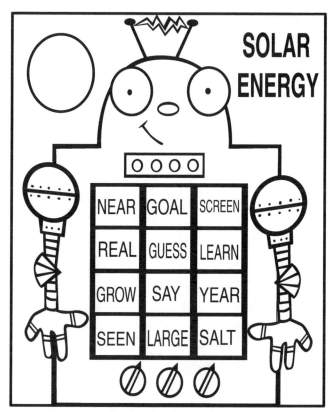

SOLAR ENERGY

NEAR	GOAL	SCREEN
REAL	GUESS	LEARN
GROW	SAY	YEAR
SEEN	LARGE	SALT

Reggie Robot runs on solar energy. Cross out any words on Reggie's screen that cannot be made from the letters in "SOLAR ENERGY." How many words are left? Write the number in the circle.

19

There are 6 things strange about this picture.
Can you find and circle them?

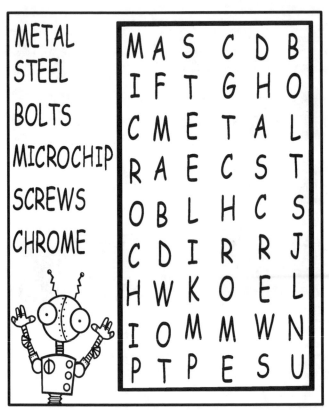

METAL
STEEL
BOLTS
MICROCHIP
SCREWS
CHROME

M	A	S	C	D	B
I	F	T	G	H	O
C	M	E	T	A	L
R	A	E	C	S	T
O	B	L	H	C	S
C	D	I	R	R	J
H	W	K	O	E	L
I	O	M	M	W	N
P	T	P	E	S	U

This list of works tells you some of the materials
from which robots can be made. Try to find them
in the box and circle them.

Help Holly the robotic cat find her way to
Rupert the Robot.

Circle the 8 things in this picture that start
with the letter "R" other than the robots.

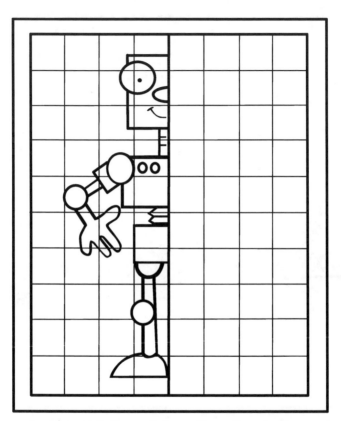

Look carefully and draw the other half
of this robot.

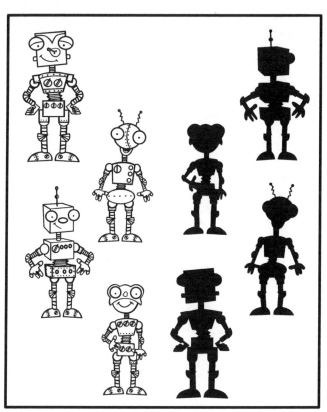

Match the robots to their shadows.

Lead Rufus through the street to his job at the factory.

Riley Robot is having sweet dreams. Can you spot a nut, a bolt, a light bulb, and a plug in his dream bubble?

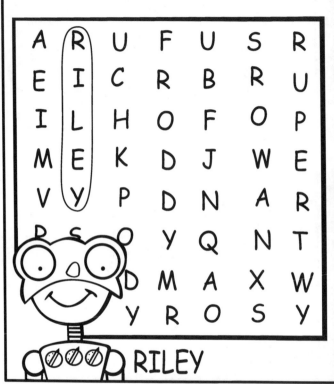

A	R	U	F	U	S	R
E	I	C	R	B	R	U
I	L	H	O	F	O	P
M	E	K	D	J	W	E
V	Y	P	D	N	A	R
D	S	O	Y	Q	N	T
	D	M	A	X	W
Y	R	O	S	Y

RILEY

First look at the pictures and names on
the opposite page. Then find those names
hidden in the box above and circle them, just
the way the name Riley is circled.

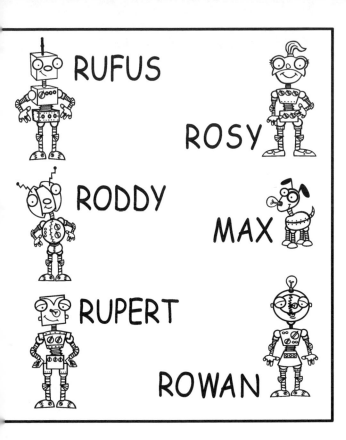

RUFUS

ROSY

RODDY

MAX

RUPERT

ROWAN

RAYMOND AND RUPERT

Cross out any words in the thought bubble that cannot be made from the letters in "Raymond and Rupert." Write the number of the words not used in the circle between them.

Riley Robot has lost 2 of his dials. Can you
find the 2 dials that match the one on his chest?

There are 10 robots hidden in this picture.
Can you find and circle the robots?

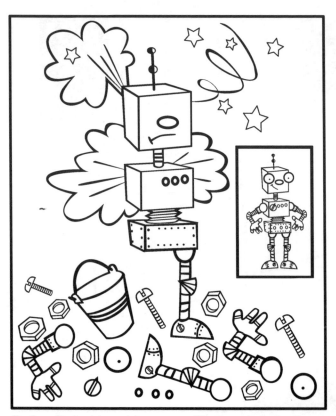

Rufus Robot has blown up. Find and circle the 7 things in the picture that belong to Rufus. Use the insert to remember what Rufus looks like.

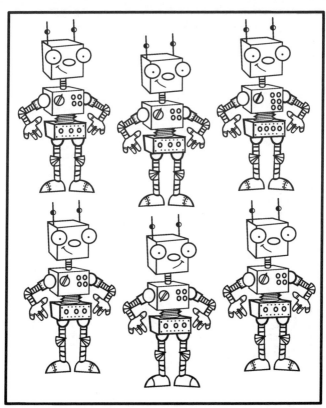

Here are 6 robots that look very much like Rufus Robot. Cross out the 2 robots that look different from the other robots.

These 2 pictures of Riley, Rosy and Max look the same, but there are 7 differences. Find and circle them on the opposite page.

38

Raymond the Robot needs 7 new nuts.
Can you circle the box that contains 7 nuts.

Lead Max and Holly the robotic pets through the maze to the park for their morning exercise.

The robotic pets enjoy a walk in the park.
Circle 10 things in this picture that start
with the letter "P" other than the pets.

B _ L _

N _ T _

P _ _ G

R _ B _ T

D _ A _

Fill in the missing letters of these items, then find and circle them in the word search on the opposite page.

44

```
R Q N A R P B
O E U B O L T
C G T D B U E
X T S F O G H
L R E I T J L
D I A L V M P
B O W U S L H
```

BROTHERS

Look at the numbered brother robots on this page. Find their look-alike sister robots on the opposite page and give them the same numbers. One is already done for you.

46

SISTERS

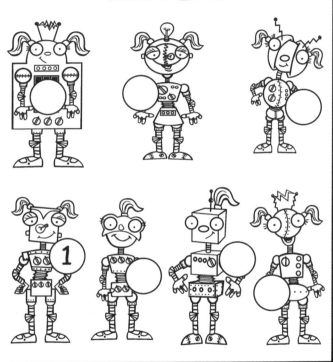

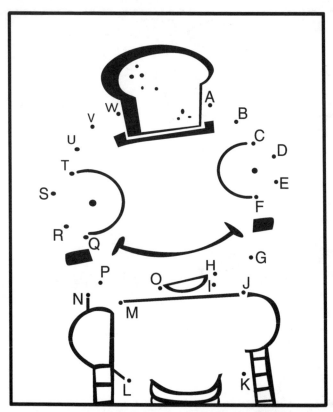

Connect the dots to see what Toastie the Robot looks like.

Here are 2 pictures of Rowan and Rose Robot.
Draw 5 things in the top picture so that it
matches the bottom one exactly.

Can you find and circle the letters that spell "ROBOTIC" within this picture.

Toastie the Robot is sitting down to his breakfast. Can you find the 12 things that start with the letter "T."

Solutions

page 4

page 5

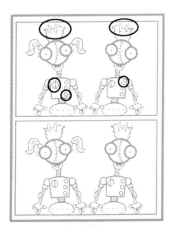

page 6

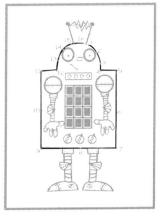

page 7

page 8

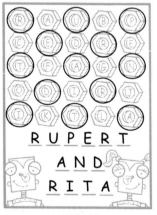

page 9

page 10

page 11

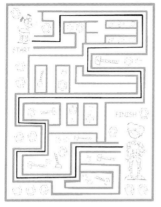

page 12

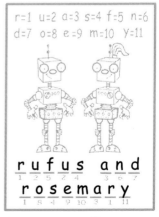

page 14

page 15

r=1 u=2 a=3 s=4 f=5 n=6
d=7 o=8 e=9 m=10 y=11

r u f u s   a n d
1 2 5 2 4   3 6 7

r o s e m a r y
1 8 4 9 10 3 1 11

page 16

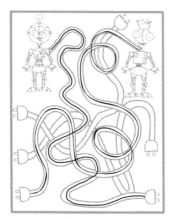

page 18

SOLAR ENERGY

(8)

NEAR	GOAL	✕
REAL	✕	LEARN
GREW	SAY	YEAR
SEEN	LARGE	✕

page 19

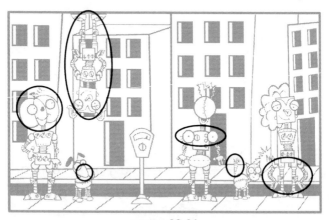

pages 20-21

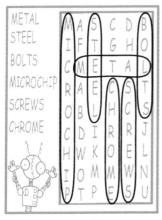

page 22

page 23

pages 24-25

rabbit, rocket, rainbow, rope, rug, rooster, ribbon and rock

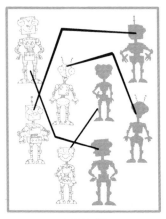

page 27

page 28

page 29

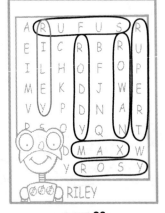

page 30

page 32

page 33

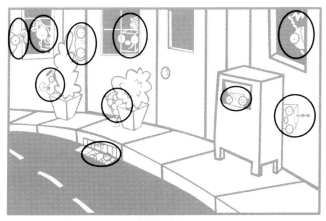

pages 34-35

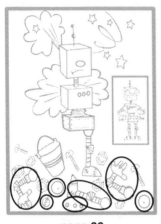

page 36

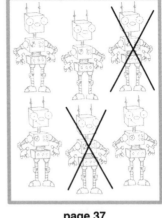

page 37

page 39

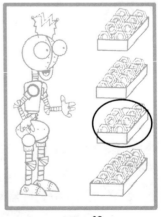

page 40

page 41

pages 42-43   pirate, pig, picnic, pie, park, parachute, puppet, pumpkin, penguin and a pine   61

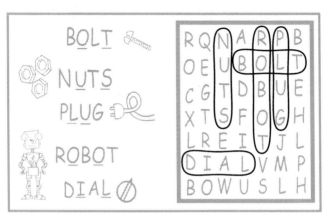

pages 44-45

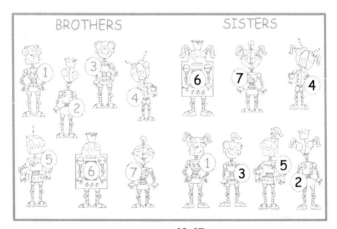

pages 46-47

page 48

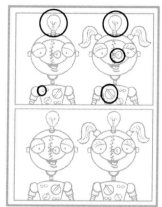

page 49

pages 50-51

page 52

triangle, two, ten, thirteen, trees,
toast, toaster, television, telephone,
teapot, thumb, a table